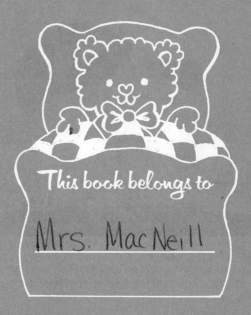

This book belongs to

Mrs. MacNeill

 An Early Start Edition from Macmillan Children's Book Clubs

First published in the United States 1990 by Chronicle Books. Copyright © 1989 by Taro Gomi.
English text copyright © 1990 by Chronicle Books. All rights reserved. First published in Japan
by Ehonkan Publishers, Tokyo. English translation rights arranged through Japan Foreign Rights
Centre.

Library of Congress Cataloging-in-Publication Data

Gomi, Tarō.
  [Minna ga oshiete kuremashita. English]
  My friends / by Taro Gomi.
      p. cm.
  Translation of: Minna ga oshiete kuremashita.
  Summary: A little girl learns to walk, climb, and study the earth from her friends, most of
whom are animals.
  [1. Growth—Fiction. 2. Animals—Fiction.] I. Title.
PZ7.G586My 1990 [E]—dc20   ISBN 0-87701-688-7   89-23940
                                                             CIP
                                                             AC

Chronicle Books, 275 Fifth Street, San Francisco, California 94103

Distributed in Canada by Raincoast Books, 112 East Third Avenue, Vancouver, B.C. V5T 1C8
            10 9 8 7 6 5 4 3 2 1

MY FRIENDS

by Taro Gomi

Chronicle Books • San Francisco

I learned to walk from my friend
the cat.

I learned to jump from my friend the dog.

I learned to climb from my friend
the monkey.

I learned to run from my friend
the horse.

I learned to march from my friend
the rooster.

I learned to nap from

my friend the crocodile.

I learned to smell the flowers
from my friend the butterfly.

I learned to hide from

my friend the rabbit.

I learned to explore the earth from

my friend the ant.

I learned to kick from my friend
the gorilla.

I learned to watch the night sky
from my friend the owl.

I learned to sing from my friends the birds.

I learned to read from

my friends the books.

I learned to study from

my friends the teachers.

I learned to play from

my friends at school.

And I learned to love from a friend like you.